Barbie™

2

Moving to the Beat

Gemma Carey

Other Barbie Sweethearts to collect:

1. Pacific Pageant

3. Butterfly Island

4. Beach Adventure

First published in Great Britain in 1996 by Reed Children's Books
Michelin House, 81 Fulham Road, London SW3 6RB
and Auckland, Melbourne, Singapore and Toronto

ISBN 0 7497 2939 2

Printed and bound in Great Britain
by Cox and Wyman Ltd, Reading, Berkshire

1 3 5 7 9 10 8 6 4 2

Contents

1

Barbie and the Dreamgirls

'Are you ready, everybody? One, two, three, four!'

Teresa clicked her drumsticks together, then began to thump out a steady ryhthm. One by one, her friends joined her. Christie led the way on the keyboards. Kira picked up the beat on her guitar. Last of all, Barbie grabbed her microphone.

'Come on!' she shouted to an invisible audience. She tossed her long, blonde hair and moved her feet in time with the music.

Pink and pretty
Get up on your feet!
Pink and pretty
Moving to the beat!

The song came to an end. The four girls put down their instruments and flopped onto the floor of Barbie's lounge.

'Phew!' puffed Teresa. 'That was really hard work.'

'It sounded brilliant, though, didn't it!'said Kira.

'You bet!' said Christie. 'It's the best song you've written so far, Barbie.'

'Thanks,' said Barbie, smiling at Christie. 'I think people might enjoy dancing to it.'

'Are you kidding?' said Kira. 'It's fantastic.' She glanced around the room they were rehearsing in. 'Too good for just these four walls. I just wish we had a chance to play it in public.'

'Me too!' echoed Teresa. 'I'd love to play on a real stage. With a proper light show, and a huge sound system . . . '

'Wouldn't we all?' agreed Christie.

Barbie looked at her friends, a secret smile pulling at her lips. Should she tell them? 'Perhaps we *can* play our songs in public . . .' she teased.

‘Huh?’ asked Kira. ‘Where? How?’

Barbie just grinned at her.

‘Do you know something *we* don’t know?’ coaxed Christie. ‘Come on, Barbie, tell us.’

‘Yes, Barbie. You know how I *hate* secrets,’ added Teresa.

‘Well,’ began Barbie, fiddling with her microphone cord. ‘You know how I do some volunteer work for the Wright Foundation.’

‘Sure,’ said Kira. ‘That’s that organisation that raises money for underprivileged kids, isn’t it?’

‘That’s right,’ said Barbie. ‘Mrs Wright is the chairperson. She’s trying to raise enough money to send a group of local kids for a holiday at the beach this summer. Some of these kids have never seen the sea, let alone gone for a holiday there,’ explained Barbie.

‘You’re kidding!’ gasped Kira. Her family went for a holiday to the beach every year. She couldn’t imagine what it was like never to have seen the sea!

'No,' said Barbie. 'It's true. That's why it's so important we raise lots of money this year.'

'Those poor kids. Of course we'd like to help them. But what's all this got to do with our band playing?' asked Christie, puzzled.

'Mrs Wright asked me to come up with some ideas for fund-raising,' explained Barbie. 'I know everyone around this neighbourhood likes listening to music, and dancing.'

'That's for sure!' cried Teresa, giving her drumstick a twirl.

'And there are lots of other bands around here like us. So I thought . . . '

'I know!' Kira cried. 'A Battle of the Bands competition!'

'Exactly,' said Barbie, smiling. 'Mrs Wright thought it was a good idea too. She's talked to the local council and they've agreed to let us use the town hall for the competition.'

'Excellent!' said Christie. 'I can just see us

up on stage now, playing "Pink and Pretty."'

'We can all wear matching pink outfits,' said Teresa. 'I saw this great little shop the other day in the shopping arcade. It's got exactly the right kind of clothes we need.'

'And we can make a big pink banner,' went on Christie, her eyes shining. 'It can say "Barbie and the Dreamgirls" in big, bold letters. And you could paint it on your bass drum, Teresa.'

'Yes,' said Teresa, just as excited. 'And . . . '

'Hang on a minute,' interrupted Kira. 'Aren't you on the organising committee for this competition, Barbie?'

'Yes,' said Barbie. 'Why?'

'Maybe Mrs Wright won't let our band enter. Other contestants might think that we'd try to rig the results.'

Barbie looked shocked. 'Oh no, Kira, I don't think so. Anyway, everything's going to be very fair. I'm only helping to *organise* the competition, not be involved in the judging.'

'That's good,' said Christie, relieved. She'd have hated to miss out on their big chance to perform in public. 'So who *is* going to be judging?' she asked.

'Mrs Wright, and her grand-children, Jessie and Todd,' said Barbie. 'They're just the right age, and they know heaps about dance music. And we've also got a special judge.'

'Who?' chorused her friends.

'Beatmaster Bob, the DJ from Radio XPY!' announced Barbie, triumphantly.

'Beatmaster Bob!' squealed Christie. 'He's the best! I *never* miss his show.'

'Wow!' sighed Teresa. 'Beatmaster Bob listening to *our* band.'

'Do you think he'll give us his autograph?' asked Christie.

Kira tossed her head. 'Hey, guys. Have some confidence! By the time we've played up on that stage, people will be queuing up to get *our* autographs!'

'Yay!' cried Teresa. 'So, Barbie. What happens

next? How do we enter?'

'We've already thought about that,' said Barbie. 'We're only able to have six or seven bands play in the competition.'

'But what if more bands than that want to go in it?' asked Christie.

'We're asking everyone to submit a demo tape with three songs on it to Beatmaster Bob,' Barbie explained. 'He'll listen to all the tapes and make a final decision. The best seven bands get to play in the final at the town hall.'

'And we'll be one of them,' said Kira softly, crossing her fingers behind her back. She thought of all the months she'd spent practising her guitar. Now there was a chance to play on a real stage in front of a real audience she didn't want to miss out!

'So we need to choose our three best songs,' went on Barbie, 'and record them on tape.'

'Pink and Pretty *has* to be one of them,' said Teresa. 'But how are we going to record them?'

'That's easy,' said Christie. 'Steve's just got a

job working as a sound engineer at Oasis Recording Studios. I'm sure he'd love to help us out.'

'Perfect!' cried Barbie. Everything was falling into place. 'And Ken can help us take all our gear over there in his van.'

'When do we start?' asked Kira, her fingers itching to get at her guitar strings.

'How about Saturday morning?' Barbie asked.

Everyone nodded.

'Great,' said Barbie. 'Christie, can you make a booking with Steve?'

Christie gave her a high five. 'You got it!'

Barbie picked up her microphone and flicked the switch. 'For now, it's back to rehearsal. Come on, Dreamgirls, let's go!'

2

The Recording Studio

Barbie pulled her pink '57 Chevy over to the kerb in front of the Oasis Recording Studio building. Kira and Teresa tumbled out.

'Wow!' breathed Teresa. 'Whoever thought we'd be spending Saturday morning in a recording studio!'

'Here come Ken and Christie with our gear,' called Kira, as a white van pulled up behind Barbie's car. Everybody helped to load musical instruments and amplifiers out of the van and into the foyer of the studio. Steve came out from behind the front desk to help them.

'Which studio?' Teresa asked him.

'Well, I booked you all into Studio One,' Steve told the group. 'It's got the best equipment.'

'Great,' said Kira. 'We're going to need it if

we want to sound good for the demo.'

'Ummm . . . there's a slight problem, though,' said Steve. 'Looks like there's already a band in Studio One. They've been there since early this morning.'

'Oh,' said Kira, disappointed. 'Can't we ask them to leave?' She studied the bookings sheet on the front desk. 'Look, it says "Barbie and the Dreamgirls" here. That's us!'

Christie tossed her long mane of dark hair. 'You did promise us Studio One, Steve. It doesn't seem very fair.'

'Hey!' said Barbie. 'I'm sure there's another studio we can use. Right, Steve?'

'Well, yes,' said Steve. 'Studio Five is free. It's not as big, but —'

'It'll be fine,' said Barbie. 'Our music will sound good in any studio. Right, Dreamgirls?'

'Right,' said Christie, smiling again. 'Who *is* the band in Studio One, Steve? Anyone famous?'

Steve shook his head. 'I don't know. They

were already recording when I arrived this morning. There's something strange going on, though.'

'Oh?' said Barbie, her ears pricking up. She loved a good mystery. 'What's that?'

'Nobody else who works round here knows what's going on, either. They must be using their own sound engineer. We haven't seen anyone come in or out. And there's a big sign on the door saying "Do Not Disturb" '.

'I wonder who it is?' said Barbie, puzzled. 'Still, we haven't got all day to worry about it. Let's get into the studio and start recording!'

Ken and Steve helped the girls load their gear onto a big trolley. They wheeled it down the corridor and into the studio.

'The walls in here are really thick,' said Teresa, looking around the room.

'The carpet and curtains are too,' explained Steve. 'They need to be, to keep the sound you make inside the studio.'

Teresa quickly set up her drum kit while

Christie and Kira organised their instruments and amplifiers. Barbie, Ken and Steve went into a little room at the back of the studio. They could see everything that was going on through a thick, glass window.

Barbie watched Steve set the levels on the mixing desk.

'We're going to record each instrument separately,' Steve explained. 'But first of all we need to make a guide track. The band will play in the studio, and we'll record you singing from in here.'

'Will my voice be on the final tape?' asked Barbie nervously.

'No,' Steve assured her. 'The guide track just helps the other musicians know what part of the song they're up to. When the instrumental track is ready, I'll get you to record your vocals over the top. If you make a mistake, you can have another try till you get it right. Okay?'

'Sounds great,' said Barbie. She settled back on the stool behind the mixing desk.

Steve flicked switches and pushed buttons as the Dreamgirls played. Barbie listened to the music coming from the studio through a set of speakers on the wall. It sounded fantastic!

When the guide track was ready, Teresa put on a set of headphones and settled herself behind the drums again. She played along to the guide track while Steve recorded her. Then it was Christie's turn on keyboards, and finally, Kira on guitar.

Barbie hummed along from her position in the recording booth. Soon her nervousness vanished. She couldn't wait until it was her turn to go into the studio.

Recording was *fun!*

3

The Mystery Band

Kira was having a great time. She loved playing guitar. She'd been practising all week, so that she would play her very best for the demo tape.

Kira climbed up onto the stool behind the mixing desk in the booth. The music she'd just played swirled into her ears through the speakers.

She watched through the window as Barbie began. 'Pink and pretty,' she sang, her mouth close to the microphone.

Steve frowned. He flicked a switch and waved to Barbie from behind the window. 'Can we start again please, Barbie?' he asked.

Barbie picked up the mike again, holding it a bit further away this time. 'Sure!' she called back.

Steve turned to Kira. 'The vocals are the hardest thing to get right,' he explained. 'This may take quite a while.'

Kira smiled back. She turned to the others. 'Anyone thirsty?'

'You bet!' said Christie.

'Me too!' said Teresa. 'I'd love a soda.'

'There's a drink machine out in the hall,' said Steve handing her a pile of change.

'Thanks,' said Kira. She wandered down the hallway till she found the drink machine. But someone had already beaten her to it.

'He looks cute,' thought Kira, watching the tall, dark guy as he searched through his pockets for coins. 'I wonder if he's a musician?'

He flicked his black, glossy curls out of his eyes and turned to Kira. 'Looks like I'm out of luck,' he said, grinning. 'I've only got notes.'

'Do you need change for the machine?' asked Kira. She held out her hand. 'I've got lots.'

'Thanks,' said the guy, handing her a note in exchange for coins. 'My name's Zac, by the way.'

'And I'm Kira,' Kira replied. Zac. His name seemed familiar. So did his face. But she was sure she'd never met him before.

Zac dropped some coins into the slot of the machine. 'Are you recording some songs here?'

'Yes,' said Kira. 'Our singer, Barbie, is recording the vocals right now.'

'Did you play too?' asked Zac.

'Sure did,' answered Kira, proudly. 'Guitar.'

'Really?' Zac smiled. 'I play bass.'

Of course, thought Kira, blushing. This was Zac Zachariah, bass player for the Purple Jets. The best dance band in the *whole* country! His band must be the mystery band in Studio One!

'Everything okay?' asked Zac, smiling.

'Y-yes,' stammered Kira. 'I'm sorry. You're Zac Zachariah, right? From the Purple Jets!'

'That's me,' said Zac. 'Do you know our music?'

'Are you kidding?' asked Kira. '*Everyone* does. My friends and I play your music all the time.'

Zac smiled again. 'So you like dance music?'

Kira nodded. 'We love it!'

'Maybe you'd like to come down to Studio One later, about five,' Zac said. 'We've just recorded some new songs. We could play them for you and you can tell us what you think.'

'Can my friends come too?' Kira asked. She knew Barbie and the rest of the gang would hate to miss out on something like this!

'Sure,' said Zac. 'We'll make it a party.' He headed off down the hallway. 'See you later then,' he called back.

Kira couldn't wait to get back to the studio to tell the others.

'Guess who I just met!' she said breathlessly, handing out cans of drink to everyone. They'd finally finished recording Barbie's vocals and were sitting round listening to the tapes.

'Who?' chorused the others.

'Remember that mystery band in Studio One?' she asked.

'The one that's using *our* studio,' Christie reminded her.

'You won't feel so bad when you know who it is,' said Kira, her eyes teasing.

'Come on, Kira, tell us!' they pleaded.

'It's the Purple Jets!' said Kira triumphantly.

'They're my favourite band!' gasped Barbie. 'I know the words to all their songs. But how do you know it's them?'

Kira told them all about how she'd met Zac at the drink machine.

'But the best thing,' she told them, 'is that he's invited us all to listen to their recording.'

'You're kidding!' said Barbie. She couldn't believe her luck. What a fantastic day this had been. She'd had the chance to record her dance songs in a proper recording studio, and now she was getting a chance to meet her favourite band. Barbie couldn't be happier.

4

Dance Party

'Pass me another slice of pizza, please Barbie,' said Teresa.

'Sure,' said Barbie. 'Pepperoni or Hawaiian?'

'Both!' laughed Teresa.

They were enjoying a well-earned lunch at Poppa's Pizza Parlour. The girls had worked hard all morning recording, and now they were starving.

'Our tape sounds fantastic,' said Christie. 'Especially your vocals, Barbie.'

Barbie smiled at her friends. 'Everyone was good.'

'This has turned out to be a great day,' said Kira. 'And we've still got more good things to happen yet.'

'That's for sure,' said Teresa, remembering Kira's invitation. 'What time did Zac say to come back to the studio, Kira?'

‘Around five,’ said Kira. ‘I can’t wait!’

‘Me either,’ said Barbie. ‘I can’t believe it! The Purple Jets! My favourite band. It was really kind of them to ask us along.’

‘Kira certainly thinks so,’ teased Christie. Kira hadn’t stopped talking about how cute their bass player had been ever since she came back from the studio.

Barbie smiled across the table at Kira. ‘I’m really glad you met up with Zac, Kira,’ she said. ‘This afternoon’s going to be great fun. But I have to go home for a while first. There’s some details about the Battle of the Bands I have to organise.’

‘See you back at the studio,’ the others called after her.

Barbie spent the afternoon writing lists of things that were needed for the band competition. It was important that things went well. The Wright Foundation needed to raise as much money as possible for the children’s holidays at the beach.

At four o'clock she put away her lists and changed her clothes. She wanted to look her best. After all, it wasn't every day she got to meet her favourite band!

Everyone else was already at the recording studios when she arrived. They all looked really excited, especially Kira.

'Come on, Barbie,' her friend urged her. 'We don't want to be late!'

Kira knocked gently on the door of Studio One. After a few moments it was opened by a pretty girl with long, white hair and violet eyes.

'Hi!' the girl greeted them. 'I'm Chantelle. You must be Kira, right?'

'Hi,' said Kira, shyly. 'These are my friends, Barbie, Teresa and Christie.'

'Hi,' said Chantelle. 'Great to meet you all. Are you coming in?' She gestured towards a lounge area at the rear of the studio. 'We've just finished. Looks like you'll be the first to hear our new album.'

'Thanks,' said Kira. 'We'd love to.' She

spotted Zac sitting on a low couch, and waved.

'Hi, Kira,' said Zac, jumping up. 'I'm glad you could make it. Come and meet the rest of the band.'

He led the four girls into the lounge area. 'This is Chantelle, who you've already met. She's our singer. And this is Jerry, who plays guitar, and BJ. He plays drums.'

Kira was suddenly overcome with shyness. Barbie took over for her friend. 'Nice to meet you all,' she said. 'I'm Barbie, and these are my friends, Teresa and Christie. And Kira, of course!'

Chantelle turned to Kira. 'Zac tells me your band plays dance music too,' she said. 'Are you the singer?'

Kira laughed. 'No, Barbie is. She writes all our songs as well.'

'Really!' said Chantelle. 'I write our songs too. I'd love to hear some of yours some time.'

'Thanks,' said Barbie. 'But it's *your* songs we've come to hear. I've got all of your albums. I play them every day. It will be a real honour to have the chance to hear your latest songs.'

'Then what are we waiting for?' asked Chantelle. 'Put the tape on, Jerry.'

Soon the studio was filled with the funky dance rhythms of the Purple Jets. Barbie couldn't keep her feet still. All she wanted to do was get up and dance. She caught Christie's eye. Christie looked like she was ready to dance as well!

The girls didn't have to wait long. Chantelle pulled Jerry up onto his feet, and began dancing energetically, her long, white hair flying. Soon everyone was dancing — Barbie with Christie, Teresa with BJ, and Kira with Zac.

Finally the music finished. Everyone fell back exhausted onto the couches. 'Now that's what I call a real dance party!' said Zac. He smiled across at Barbie. 'Did you like our music?'

'It was fantastic,' said Barbie. 'Your new songs are even better than your old ones!'

'Thanks,' said Zac. 'That's good to hear.

We're going on tour soon, to promote our new album.'

'Great!' said Barbie. Barbie loved the excitement of travelling. Touring sounded like fun. 'When do you leave?'

'Not for a few weeks,' said Zac. 'We're just waiting for our tour manager to finalise all the details.'

The music started up again and Zac asked Christie to dance this time. Barbie sat quietly watching them.

'What's up, Barbie?' asked Teresa, sitting down next to her friend. 'You look very serious. Is something the matter?'

Barbie turned towards Teresa, her blue eyes shining. 'I've just had the most fantastic idea!' she cried.

5

Barbie's Big Idea

Teresa could tell by the look in Barbie's eyes that she was planning something pretty big. 'Well, what's your fantastic idea?' she asked. 'Something to do with the competition, I bet!'

Barbie's blue eyes danced. 'It sure is,' she said. 'It's probably the best idea I've had all week.'

'So come on,' begged Teresa. 'Tell us!'

'Well,' began Barbie. 'I've been thinking about the Wright Foundation, and how we need to raise as much money as we can.'

'But you've already organised the Battle of the Bands,' pointed out Teresa. 'Lots of people will come to see that.'

'True,' said Barbie. 'But all the bands performing will be local bands. Not many of them will be very well known.'

'Go on,' said Teresa.

‘If we had a really famous band playing, as a special guest act, lots of people would want to come. We’d sell heaps of tickets and raise even more money.’

Teresa frowned. ‘True. But we don’t know any famous bands.’

Barbie grinned. She pointed at Christie, dancing with Zac. ‘Not until today we didn't!’

‘Barbie, you’re a genius! Do you really think the Purple Jets would want to play at our fund-raiser, though?’

‘Well, we can only ask,’ said Barbie. ‘They seem like nice people. And when we explain what it’s for, I’m sure they’ll want to help.’

‘I hope so,’ said Teresa. She watched as Zac spun Christie around in time to the music. ‘Come on, Barbie. It isn’t every day we get our own private dance party with a famous dance band. Let’s dance!’

Soon everyone in the room was up on their feet again. This time, though, they were dancing to one of the Purple Jets’ earlier records. As she danced, Barbie sang along.

Party time

Got to shake and move

It's party time

Got to get into the groove.

Chantelle and Jerry stopped dancing for a moment to listen to Barbie singing. 'Hey!' said Chantelle admiringly. 'You're pretty good.'

'Thanks,' Barbie smiled back.

'Maybe we could do a duet some time,' said Chantelle. 'Our voices are very similar.'

Barbie smiled modestly. 'I'd love to. But do you really think I'm good enough?'

'Are you kidding?' said Chantelle. 'You're great! Anything I can help you with, just let me know.'

Teresa flashed a look at Barbie. Barbie nodded. This was the perfect time to ask.

Barbie explained to the band all about the Wright Foundation, and what they were planning to do that summer. As soon as the Purple Jets found out that all the money raised would go to help kids needing holidays, they were eager to help out.

'Poor kids,' said Chantelle. 'Of course we'll play a few numbers, won't we, guys?'

The rest of the band nodded. 'I'll even get the staging and lighting guys to put on a special lighting show,' said Zac. 'Just like we have for our shows when we go on tour. It'll be fun.'

'It'll be sort of like a "pre-tour show,"' added Jerry. 'We can find out what's going to work well with an audience before we go on tour, and help you guys out at the same time.'

Barbie's eyes shone. The Purple Jets, the best dance band in the country, were going to play at her fund-raiser! Now everyone in town would want to come. They were sure to sell lots of tickets. She couldn't wait to tell Mrs Wright and the other members of the foundation the exciting news.

6

The Phone Call

'Do you think Beatmaster Bob will like our tape?' Kira asked Barbie.

'Let's hope so,' said Barbie. 'We just have to make it into the final now the Purple Jets are going to be playing.'

The girls were standing in the comfortable foyer of Radio XPY. The carpet was thick and plush under their feet. The wood-panelled walls were covered with photos of the various DJs.

'Look,' said Kira. She pointed to a picture of a young guy with fair hair tied back in a pony tail, and a crinkly smile. 'There's a picture of Beatmaster Bob. He's kind of cute, isn't he!'

'I thought it was Zac you thought was cute,' Barbie teased her.

Kira gave her friend a playful swat.

'Can I help you?' asked the receptionist, putting down the phone. Her face was stern.

'Hi,' said Barbie, putting on a serious face. 'We're from Barbie and the Dreamgirls. We've come to enter our tape in the Battle of the Bands competition.'

The receptionist waved her hand in the direction of a large box. 'Just leave your tape along with the others, please, girls,' she said. 'Bob will pick them all up at the end of the day.'

Barbie placed their tape in the box. She was dismayed to see that it was almost full. Lots of bands must be trying out for the competition!

'Oh well,' she said to Kira. 'Even if we don't get chosen, at least we know the fund-raiser will be a success. Mrs Wright will be really pleased.'

'That's for sure,' said Kira. 'Come on, let's go and meet the others.'

The girls had arranged to meet at Poppa Carlo's for pizza. Barbie wanted to fill them in with more details about the fund-raiser. She needed as much help as she could get to make the big night a success, and she knew she could count on her friends. They were a team!

Teresa made space for Barbie and Kira at the table. 'How was Radio XPY?' she asked.

'Did you get to meet Beatmaster Bob?' asked Christie excitedly, before Barbie or Kira had a chance to answer.

'No,' said Barbie. 'But we saw his picture, didn't we, Kira!'

'Sure did,' said Kira, picking up the menu. 'I can't wait to meet him.'

'He just has to choose our tape,' sighed Christie. 'When will we find out?'

'Probably not until the end of the week,' said Barbie. 'There was a huge box of tapes for him to listen to.'

'I'll never be able to wait that long,' sighed Kira. 'What can we do to take our mind off it?'

'Well,' said Barbie thoughtfully. 'You can help me out, if you like. There's a million things to do to get ready for the fund-raiser. We need to make posters, and send out invitations to important people like the mayor and her husband.'

'Great!' said Christie. 'I love making posters. Then we can go round to all the shops and schools in the area and ask if we can put them up in the windows!'

We'll need to think about how we can decorate the town hall too,' said Teresa. 'I've got some great ideas! We can have bunches of purple balloons and streamers everywhere, in honour of our special guest act.'

'And cardboard models of purple jets!' put in Kira.

Barbie smiled at her friends' enthusiasm. Between the four of them, they'd get lots of things done. She knew she'd be able to count on them!

For the next few days, the girls were too busy writing lists and designing posters and invitations to worry too much about whether or not their tape had been chosen.

The local shop-keepers had been very generous when they found out why the band competition was being organised, and donated all sorts of things like food, bottles of pop and decorations. The manager of the local discount store had even offered to donate prizes to the finalists in the competition.

On the following Saturday, Barbie and her friends met for their regular lunch at Poppa's. They crowded into their favourite booth and ordered pizzas with the lot.

'Pheww!' said Teresa, tucking into a large slice. 'Christie and I must have put up about thirty posters this morning. I really feel like I've earned this!'

'Me too,' groaned Kira. 'I spent all morning licking envelopes.' She stuck her tongue out of her mouth. 'I can still taste the glue!'

Barbie laughed. Her own fingers were aching from folding up hundreds of flyers announcing the band competition. 'But it's all been for a good cause. Mrs Wright was thrilled when I told her about all the things the local shop-keepers have donated.'

The girls munched contentedly for a while. 'I don't suppose you've heard anything yet about our tape?' asked Christie hopefully.

Barbie shook her head. 'Not yet. I expect we won't hear anything till next week now.'

'Hey, listen to what's on the radio!' cried Kira. The girls turned their heads to listen to the sounds swirling through the pizza parlour.

'Party time, got to shake and move,' sang a familiar voice.

'Hey!' said Teresa. 'It's Chantelle!'

'The Purple Jets!' chorused Barbie and Christie.

They listened to the song, their eyes shining. Last time they'd heard it, they'd actually been in a studio with the band who was singing it!

'It must be an omen,' breathed Kira, when the song finished.

'Oh, I hope so,' said Christie. 'It would be fun to see those guys again!'

Poppa Carlo suddenly appeared at their table. 'I'm sorry to interrupt your fun, girls,' he said. 'Barbie, can you come out to the kitchen for a minute,' he asked softly.

Barbie was mystified. 'Sure, Poppa Carlo. Is something wrong?'

Poppa Carlo smiled at her gently. 'I hope not, Barbie. It's Ken on the phone. He wants to talk to you. He said it was urgent.'

Barbie held her breath. An urgent phone call? From Ken? What on earth could it be?

7

Pink and Pretty

'Hello? Ken? It's me, Barbie.' Barbie tried to keep any signs of worry out of her voice. Maybe her sister Skipper had had an accident!

'Barbie?' Ken's voice sounded excited. 'I've got some good news for you!'

'You have?' Barbie relaxed.

'Skipper just rang me, trying to find out where you are,' Ken informed her. 'I had a feeling you might all be down at Poppa's by now. It seems someone from Radio XPY has been trying to get in touch with you.'

Barbie held her breath again. 'They have? Did Skipper say what it was about?'

'She sure did. Looks like your wish has come true. Your band has been chosen to be one of the finalists at the Battle of the Bands.'

Barbie gave a little squeal of excitement. They were in! 'Thanks for letting me know,

Ken. I can't wait to tell the others!'

'Fantastic!' cried her friends when they heard the news. They bombarded Barbie with question after question:

'What will we wear?'

'How should we do our hair?'

'How will we ever get our act ready in time?'

'Which song do you think we should play?'

Barbie held her hands up in mock dismay. 'One at a time!' she laughed.

'Well, I think we should definitely play "Pink and Pretty,"' said Kira. 'It's our best song.'

'I know!' said Christie. 'Why don't we work out some dance steps to go with it? Then, people are sure to want to dance along with us!'

'Good idea!' said Barbie. 'And now that we know we are definitely in the competition, we can do some of those other things we talked about.'

'You mean like making a banner with our name on it,' said Christie.

'And painting "Barbie and the Dreamgirls"

on my bass drum,' added Teresa.

'That's the idea, Teresa,' said Barbie. 'We should wear matching outfits too. Didn't you say you saw some cute ones in the arcade?'

'That's right,' said Teresa. 'In that new boutique next to the soda fountain.'

Barbie's eyes sparkled. 'Come on, girls, we deserve a treat after all our hard work. Let's go shopping!'

The girls piled into Barbie's car and set off for the arcade. 'Pink and pretty' they sang, as they cruised off round the corner, making passers-by stare at the group of pretty, lively girls, singing their hearts out in a bright-pink car.

Teresa led them through the maze of shops at the arcade to the new boutique.

The inside of the shop made the girls feel like they'd stepped right inside the pages of a fashion magazine. There were mirrors in gilt frames lining the walls, coloured lights hanging from the ceiling, and sparkling white tiles on the floor. Eveywhere they looked were racks and racks of the most gorgeous outfits.

'What do you think, Barbie?' asked Kira, holding up a yellow micro mini with a matching jacket.

'That would look great on you,' agreed Barbie. 'But look at this. Isn't it darling?' She held up a pale-pink knitted dress with tiny pearls around the neckline.

'These would look great on stage!' cried Christie, burrowing through a pile of clothes on a display table. She waved a pair of silvery lurex leggings at them.

The shop assistant came over. 'Can I be of any help?' she asked politely.

'Thanks,' said Barbie. 'We're all in a band. We need some outfits to wear for our first-ever stage appearance.'

The shop assistant frowned. 'Hmmm. A band. Something to make you stand out?'

'Definitely!' chorused the girls.

'What's the name of your band?' she

asked.

'Barbie and the Dreamgirls,' Kira answered.

'I've got some lovely new outfits that have just come in from Paris,' the assistant suggested. 'Come and have a look.'

As soon as the girls saw the clothes, they knew they were exactly right for them.

'Look at these,' cried Kira. She held up a pair of hot-pink leggings, with a matching t-shirt. 'Pink *and* pretty! Get it?'

'We could wear these minidresses over the top,' said Barbie. There were four or five little dresses on the rack, in different colours. Each had tiny straps and a short, flared skirt, and was decorated with swirls of pink and gold.

'Shoes?' suggested Christie.

'No problem,' said the shop assistant helpfully.

She showed them a display of soft leather ankle boots with white laces. 'You could always exchange the white laces for pink ones, to match your leggings and tops.'

'That's a great idea,' said Barbie. 'Thanks so much for your help.'

'Any time,' smiled the shop assistant. 'There's just one condition!'

'What's that?' asked Barbie.

'You have to tell me where you're playing,' she said, her brown eyes twinkling. 'I'd love to see all my clothes up on stage!'

'You've got it!' laughed Barbie. 'As long as you bring lots of friends!'

8

The Big Night

'Have you got everything?' Ken asked. 'Okay, let's go!'

The big night had finally arrived. Ken's van was loaded with the Dreamgirls' instruments and equipment. They were off to the town hall!

The girls had spent all afternoon putting the finishing touches on their act. They'd worked out a sensational dance routine, and they'd rehearsed their song till they could have played it backwards in their sleep. Now, it was time for the show!

Ken parked his van round the side of the hall and helped the girls unload their gear into the room at the back of the stage. The hall was a hive of activity. The band competition was only an hour away, and stagehands were running around checking lights and sound equipment.

Barbie made sure their own equipment was

safe, then rushed off in search of Mrs Wright.

'There you are, Barbie,' called Mrs Wright. Her kind eyes crinkled with delight at the preparations going on in the town hall. It was the best she'd seen it looking for years.

'Come and meet my grand-children, Jessie and Todd.' She introduced Barbie to a young boy and girl, of about Skipper's age. They both had blonde hair and smiling faces.

'Looking forward to judging the band competition?' Barbie asked them

'You bet!' said Jessie. 'I *love* dance music.'

'And the Purple Jets are my favourite band,' confided Todd.

'Mine too!' said Barbie. 'Aren't we lucky!'

'Luck had nothing to do with it,' chortled Mrs Wright. 'You're a very clever young woman, Barbie. I don't know how you managed to pull this whole thing together, but it looks like it's worked. We've completely sold out of tickets.'

'Really!' cried Barbie, her eyes shining.

'That's fabulous! It looks like those kids are going to get a really great holiday this year.'

'Well, if they do, it's all thanks to you, Barbie,' said Mrs Wright. 'Good luck in the competition.'

Barbie made some last minute checks with other members of the organising committee, and made sure that the judging panel, including Beatmaster Bob, had comfortable seats with a good view of the stage. Then she hurried backstage to join her friends. The audience had started to arrive.

The Dreamgirls were busy changing into their hot-pink outfits.

'What's happening out there, Barbie?' asked Teresa.

'Oh, everything looks great,' enthused Barbie, slipping her t-shirt over her head.

'Has Beatmaster Bob arrived yet?' asked Kira.

'Yes,' said Barbie. 'All the judges are in place.'

'What about the Purple Jets?' asked Christie,

tuning her guitar carefully. 'Are they here yet?'

'All their equipment is here,' said Barbie. 'And the special lighting show and everything. But, no, I haven't actually seen any of the band members yet. Oh, dear.'

'Don't worry, Barbie,' Kira assured her. 'They're probably just running late.' She looked at her watch. 'What time does the show start?'

'In three minutes,' said Barbie excitedly. 'Come on, Dreamgirls, let's wish each other good luck!'

'That's the spirit!' said Kira. 'We're the greatest!'

The four girls gave each other big hugs, then moved to the wings at the side of the stage so they could watch the first act. It was a rock band called Outer Space. They weren't too bad, but the girls knew they could play much better.

The next band, The Funky Chickens, was fantastic! Like the Dreamgirls, the band members were all dressed in matching outfits, and their song had a really good beat. The audience seemed to think so too. When the band finished they whistled and cheered.

Finally it was time for Barbie and the Dreamgirls to play. Barbie took her place up on stage, in front of the band. She looked out into the audience, trying to spot Ken and Steve, but the lights dazzled her eyes.

Teresa began counting in the band with her drumsticks. Barbie picked up her microphone confidently. This was their big chance. She just had to sing well!

Pink and pretty

Get up on your feet!

Pink and pretty

Moving to the beat!

The three girls danced along the stage. One, two, three, kick! Back, two, three, kick! At the end of the song, the crowd burst into wild applause and cheers.

Barbie turned to her friends, her eyes shining. 'You were great, girls!'

'So were you, Barbie!' said Kira. The four girls ran backstage, jumping with excitement. They'd finally achieved their ambition — to play on a real stage, to a real audience. And the crowd had loved them!

'Do you think the judges liked us?' Teresa asked anxiously.

'I hope so,' said Christie. 'That other band was pretty good, remember.'

'All that matters is that we played our best,' said Barbie. 'Come on, girls, let's go back out into the hall with the others and find out what they thought.'

9

The Missing Band

Ken, Steve and Skipper were waiting for Barbie and Christie in the hall.

'You were great, Barbie,' said Skipper. 'All my friends thought your song was fantastic! Some of them even asked me if I could get them your autograph.'

'Thanks, Skipper,' said Barbie. 'I'm glad you enjoyed our act.'

'I think the judges did too,' said Ken, giving Barbie a hug. 'They were all smiling while you were playing, anyway.'

'What happens now?' asked Kira.

'Well, first of all we have the judging,' Barbie explained. 'Mrs Wright and other members of the foundation will make a few speeches. And then we have the special event that everyone's waiting for. The Purple Jets!'

'Great!' said Kira. She was looking forward

to seeing Zac again.

'Are they here yet, Barbie?' asked Teresa. 'I can't see them in the hall anywhere. And we know they weren't backstage.'

Barbie looked around, a concerned expression on her face. She checked her watch. Only half an hour before they were due to play. What was holding them up?

Ken noticed her alarm. 'Don't worry, Barbie,' he assured her. 'I'll wait at the front of the hall and keep a look out for them. You go and enjoy yourself with the rest of the band. It's time for the judging.'

Barbie gave him a kiss on the cheek. 'Thanks, Ken. That's really kind of you.'

The noise of people talking in the hall gradually died down as Mrs Wright took her place in front of the microphone on the stage. She cleared her throat and began her speech.

'I'd like to welcome you all to our Battle of the Bands competition,' she said. 'Many people have worked very hard over the last few weeks to put this event together. But there's one person in the room tonight I'd like to thank especially.'

'She's probably going to thank Beatmaster Bob,' Barbie whispered to Kira. 'He's put in a lot of time judging the tapes and things.'

Mrs Wright held up a large bunch of flowers. 'I'd like you all to welcome to the stage . . . Barbie!'

Barbie gasped. Mrs Wright wanted to thank *her*. In front of all these people! She proudly walked up the steps onto the stage and stood beside Mrs Wright in the spotlight. The cheers from the audience rang in her ears.

'Thanks, everyone,' said Barbie, her eyes shining. 'But I couldn't have done any of this work without the help of my friends. Let's all give them a big hand!'

The audience clapped and cheered once again. Barbie returned to her seat, her heart bursting with pride.

'Thanks, Barbie,' smiled Mrs Wright. 'Now we come to the exciting part of the evening. The judging. I'd like everyone to meet our celebrity judge for the evening, Beatmaster Bob, from Radio XPY.'

Beatmaster Bob took his place on stage next to Mrs Wright. He spoke for a few minutes about how much he'd enjoyed listening to the tapes, and how proud he was to be able to help out such a worthy cause. Then he said the words everyone was waiting to hear. 'And now, for the winners!'

A hush fell over the room. The Dreamgirls double-crossed their fingers and held their breath.

'Third place goes to . . . The Cruisers,' announced Beatmaster Bob. Everyone clapped and cheered as the band members walked up on stage to collect their prize.

'And now for the winners of the evening,' said Beatmaster Bob. The room quietened again. 'The standard was very high tonight, and it was very hard for the judges to choose between first and second place. But our final selection was . . . The Funky Chickens, with Barbie and the Dreamgirls runners up!'

Once again, the audience clapped and cheered. Kira turned to Barbie, her pretty face crumpling with disappointment.

'Runners up?' she cried. 'Oh, Barbie, I *know* we were better than that other band! I wanted so much to win!'

'We *did* play well,' said Christie. 'I thought we had a good chance of winning too.'

'After all that work,' sighed Teresa. 'Oh well.'

'Hey!' said Barbie, giving her best and brightest smile. 'We had fun, didn't we-rehearsing and choosing our outfits?

Her friends nodded. It *had* been fun.

'Winning isn't everything,' said Barbie. 'What's more important is that we had a good time trying. And think of how much money we've raised for those kids. That's what really matters here.'

'You're right, Barbie,' said Teresa. 'Come on, Dreamgirls, let's go up and collect our prize.'

The girls waited till The Funky Chickens had finished their acceptance speech, then bounced up onto the stage.

The crowd whistled and stamped their feet. 'Go, Dreamgirls!' they cheered.

A hush fell over the crowd again. Now that the judging was finished, they were waiting for the highlight of the evening — the Purple Jets!

Barbie scanned the hall, looking for any sign of Ken or members of the missing band. What if they didn't show up? All these people who'd paid their money and come along expecting to see the famous band would be let down. It simply couldn't happen!

Ken suddenly appeared at her side.

'Any news?' asked Barbie quickly.

'None, I'm afraid,' Ken told her sadly. 'It looks like your friends have let you down.'

Barbie sighed, and looked towards the stage. The curtains were closed. A single purple spotlight shone on them, waiting to light up the band as soon as they opened. Whispers of anticipation broke out from the crowd as they waited patiently for the band to start playing. Barbie was really worried now. The crowd wouldn't wait patiently forever. If only she knew what was causing the delay. Or . . . whether the Purple Jets were going to turn up at all!

10

Barbie Saves the Day

'Hey!' said Ken, suddenly. 'Isn't that Kira over by the side door? She looks like she's trying to get our attention.'

'Maybe she's heard some news,' said Barbie, hurrying over to her friend who was waving frantically from the side of the stage.

'What's happening?' said Barbie.

'Well, I've got good news and bad news, I'm afraid,' said Kira. Christie and Teresa stood beside her, looking worried.

'Is it about the Purple Jets?' asked Barbie. 'Are they here?

'Yes,' her friend told her. 'That's the *good* news.'

'Well, let's get them up on stage then,' said Barbie. 'The audience is waiting.'

'Well, then there's the bad news,' said Kira. 'They had a car accident on the way here.'

'Oh no!' cried Barbie. 'Was anyone hurt?'

'It wasn't a serious one,' said Kira. 'But –'

She broke off as Zac arrived. 'Hi, Barbie,' he said. 'Sorry we're late.'

'That's okay,' said Barbie. 'As long as you're all here now. Can you get started right away?'

Zac looked at Kira. 'You haven't told her?'

'Told me what?' said Barbie, looking worried.

'It's Chantelle. She hit her head when we had the accident. Nothing serious, but she's very shaken and upset. She doesn't think she'll be able to go on stage and sing.'

'Oh, poor Chantelle,' said Barbie.

'I'm so sorry, Barbie,' said Zac. 'The hall looks great. You must have done a lot of work. Maybe next year.'

'Zac,' said Kira. 'The rest of you are okay, aren't you? You can still play?'

'Yes,' said Zac. 'We're fine. Why?'

'I've just had a great idea,' smiled Kira. '*Barbie* can sing!'

'What!' cried Barbie.

'Go on, Barbie, you'll be great!' said Teresa.

'I . . . I couldn't,' stammered Barbie. 'Not with The Purple Jets.'

'But you know the words to their songs,' Christie pointed out. 'Remember that day in the studio. You did just fine. Didn't she, Zac?'

'You were great, Barbie,' Zac encouraged her. 'We'd love you to sing with us anytime.' Barbie looked at her friends' faces, then back at the crowd waiting patiently for the highlight of the evening to begin.

'Come on, Barbie,' said Kira. 'Think of how much it would mean to Mrs Wright and the other members of the Foundation.'

'Besides,' said Christie. 'You're a great singer. Everyone knows that!'

'The band will be behind you all the way,' said Zac.

'Okay,' said Barbie. 'I'll do it!'

'Yay!' cried her friends, giving her a hug. 'You're the greatest, Barbie!'

Moments later, Barbie was up on stage,

surrounded by Zac, Jerry and BJ. Chantelle gave her a little wave of encouragement from her seat in the wings.

Barbie listened to the introduction to the first song, and taking a deep breath, began to sing.

Party time

Got to shake and move

Party time

Got to get into the groove.

She looked out at the audience. People had jumped out of their seats and were dancing in the aisles and in front of the stage.

The Purple Jets played five more songs. Barbie sang them all brilliantly. At the end of their set, the crowd called for an encore.

Finally, it was all over. Kira and the rest of the gang crowded into the dressing room back stage.

'You were fantastic, Barbie,' cried Christie. 'You sang really well!'

'You looked really great up there on stage,'

said Teresa. 'Maybe you should make a career out of singing.'

Chantelle and Jerry, who'd been sitting in a corner quietly talking, looked up and smiled.

'We thought so, too,' said Jerry. 'In fact, we've got a special question to ask you, Barbie.'

'We were wondering if you would like to join our band,' said Chantelle.

'You mean, join The Purple Jets!' gasped Barbie.

'Sure,' said Zac. 'You'd be great. You and Chantelle could share the vocals. Your voices would sound really great together.'

Barbie was stunned. The best dance band in the country wanted her to join their act!

'It would be a fantastic opportunity for you, Barbie,' said Kira.

Barbie's mind was spinning. It would be great to travel around the country with a famous band. But what about her own band, Barbie and the Dreamgirls? Her friends had helped her when she needed them. It would be wrong to turn her back on them now.

She turned to Chantelle and Jerry. 'Thanks, guys,' she said. 'I had a great time tonight, and I'd really love to join your group. But I think I'd rather stay with my own band.' She looked around at her friends. 'That is if the Dreamgirls want me to.'

Her friends laughed. 'Of course we do, Barbie. You're the greatest!'

Ken moved forward and gave her a big hug. 'That's for sure, Barbie.'

Barbie smiled. 'It's nice to know I've got such great friends. Come on, everybody. Let's party!'